HOME ALONE

HOME ALONE

ELEANOR SCHICK

THE DIAL PRESS · NEW YORK

Published by
The Dial Press
1 Dag Hammarskjold Plaza
New York, New York 10017

Library of Congress Cataloging in Publication Data
Schick, Eleanor. 1942– Home alone.
Summary: A young boy spends his first afternoon
alone at home while his mother is at work.
[1. Self-reliance—Fiction.
2. Mothers—Employment—Fiction] I. Title.
PZ7.S3445Ho [E] 79-19785
ISBN 0-8037-4256-8 lib. bdg.
ISBN 0-8037-4255-X pbk.

The art for each picture consists of
a pencil drawing and three halftone separations.

For Laura O. Dorfman,

whose idea it was, twenty years ago

CONTENTS

1 / Coming Home   9

2 / Home Alone   17

3 / Not So Alone   31

4 / Doing a Good Job   41

5 / Waiting for Mom   47

8

1

COMING HOME

I have walked home

from school alone before.

I do that almost every day.

But today it is different.

Today my mother

started working all day.

That is why

she will not be there

when I get home from school.

I have my own keys.

The bigger key

is for the downstairs door.

I have practiced using them

with Mom so I know how.

Some days after school

I will be going to Scout meetings.

Some days I will be visiting

with Tony or Jerry or David.

Some days I will be playing soccer

with the soccer team.

Those days Mom will pick me up

on her way home from work

because I am not allowed

to walk home alone

when it is dark.

But some days I will be coming
right home from school by myself.
That's all right with me.

Mrs. Scott lives right next door.
She will be there
if I need her for anything
or if I just get lonely
and want to visit.
She hears me
coming up the stairs,
and she opens the door
to say hello.

She says

she will be home

all afternoon.

2

HOME ALONE

I have to lock the door
when I come in
even before I call Bisquits.
I promised Dad I would.

Next I call Mom at her office
to say that I am home.

She is glad to hear that

I locked the door right away.

I tell her I remember

that if someone knocks,

I will not let them in.

I will tell them,

"Mom is busy. Come back later."

Mom says there is a note
on the bookcase in the hall.
She tells me she loves me,
and she will be home at six.

I find the note. It says:

"Dear Andy—

Welcome home!

The cookies on the kitchen table
are for you.

Also, take a glass of milk.

Remember to do your homework.

And please take the hamburgers
out of the freezer
so we can have them for dinner.

I'll see you at six.

I love you!

Love, Mom"

I fold the note

and put it in my pocket.

I can look at it again

to remember

all the things

I have to do.

I hear footsteps

on the stairs

in the hall

outside our door.

They sound louder

than they ever did before.

Bisquits says

it is just

someone coming home.

The sound of a key

turning in a lock

surprises me.

It is so loud,

it sounds like someone

is opening our door.

I look through the peephole

and see that it is just Mrs. Sherman

across the hall,

coming home from shopping.

Bisquits says she knew that

all the time.

The rooms are bigger

when there is no one here

but Bisquits and me.

We walk through the house.

It is very quiet.

The only sound is my footsteps.

We go into the kitchen.

It is time to have cookies.

Bisquits is hungry too.

Bisquits says

she is used to being home alone.

Sometimes she has to wait for us
all day, and she does not mind.
If Bisquits can stay home alone,
then I can too.

3

NOT SO ALONE

I have even more friends

besides Bisquits

who wait for me at home.

They do not worry.

They know I will play with them
when I get here.

Today I will build a town for them!

It will keep them

warm and safe

in the daytime

while they wait for me.

I take my radio off the night table.

I put it in the middle of the town.

The animals gather around it.

They think it is magic.

They say

they like the music this town has

and they like the magic music box.

Now they do not have to hear
the stairs creaking in the hallway
whenever someone comes home.

The tower has a clock
so the animals can tell
what time it is.

Right now

they are helping me

watch for six o'clock.

A train drives into town.

One of the cars has cookies in it.

The train is bringing cookies

to the animals.

The animals are having a party
because they like the new town.

4

DOING A GOOD JOB

The phone rings.

I say "Hello."

The lady asks for my mother.

I say,

"My mother will

call you back.

Can I take a message?"

The lady says "Yes."

She spells out her name

so I can write it down.

She tells me

her phone number

to write down too.

Then she thanks me

and says "Good-bye."

Bisquits thinks

I did that very well.

> Dear mom,
>   mrs. Franklin called.
>   She wants you to
> call her back.
>   Call 661-2326
>   Love, Andy

I put the note on the kitchen table
under the sugar bowl.
I remember the hamburgers
and take them out of the freezer.

I do my last page of homework.

I wash the glass I used for milk.

Then I look out the window.

The dark shadows

mean night is coming.

5

WAITING FOR MOM

Bisquits and I

count the lights

in the windows

across the street.

The animals are resting now.

They had a good day.

Bisquits is cuddly.

She likes our new town.

Bisquits says

the animals hope

we can keep this town

for a long time.

Bisquits says

maybe Mom will not mind,

if I promise

to keep my room

very clean.

It is almost six o'clock.

Mom gets home

even before she said she would!

I show Mom the town I built,

with the clock in the tower

and the magic music box.

"It is beautiful," Mom says.

"Can I leave it up

for a few days

if I promise

to keep my room clean?" I ask.

"Yes," she says,

"if you keep your promise."

I show her the note

about Mrs. Franklin.

I show her the hamburgers

defrosting for dinner.

Mom says I did a good job,
and she is very proud of me.

I tell her about the lemon seeds

we planted in school today

and the candy dish

I am making out of clay.

Mom tells me about her new office.

She says, "It will look wonderful

with a lemon plant and a candy dish."

"And I will draw some pictures

to put up on your office walls!"

I tell her.

Mom says,

"That will make it just perfect!"

I set the table,

while Mom starts cooking dinner.

"We'll have potatoes and a salad

to go with the hamburgers," she says.

"And there is still time,

while dinner is cooking,

for you to take your bath,"

she tells me.

But first she lets me peek

at the lemon cake

that she brought home for dessert.

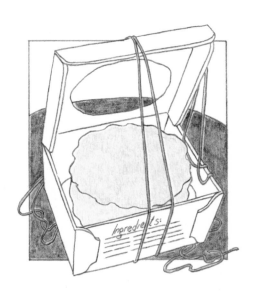